A Note to Parents and Caregivers:

Read-it! Readers are for children who are just starting on the amazing road to reading. These beautiful books support both the acquisition of reading skills and the love of books.

The PURPLE LEVEL presents basic topics and objects using high frequency words and simple language patterns.

The RED LEVEL presents familiar topics using common words and repeating sentence patterns.

The BLUE LEVEL presents new ideas using a larger vocabulary and varied sentence structure.

The YELLOW LEVEL presents more challenging ideas, a broad vocabulary, and wide variety in sentence structure.

The GREEN LEVEL presents more complex ideas, an extended vocabulary range, and expanded language structures.

The ORANGE LEVEL presents a wide range of ideas and concepts using challenging vocabulary and complex language structures.

When sharing a book with your child, read in short stretches, pausing often to talk about the pictures. Have your child turn the pages and point to the pictures and familiar words. And be sure to reread favorite stories or parts of stories.

There is no right or wrong way to share books with children. Find time to read with your child, and pass on the legacy of literacy.

Adria F. Klein, Ph.D.
Professor Emeritus
California State University
San Bernardino, California

Editor: Jill Kalz
Designer: Lori Bye
Page Production: Melissa Kes
Art Director: Nathan Gassman
Associate Managing Editor: Christianne Jones
The illustrations in this book were created digitally.

Picture Window Books
151 Good Counsel Drive
P.O. Box 669
Mankato, MN 56002-0669
877-845-8392
www.picturewindowbooks.com

Printed in the United States of America.

Library of Congress Cataloging-in-Publication Data
Loewen, Nancy, 1964-
Gordon Grizwald's grumpy goose / by Nancy Loewen ; illustrated by
Justin Greathouse.
p. cm. — (Read-it! readers: tongue twisters)
ISBN-13: 978-1-4048-4878-8 (library binding)
[1. Tongue twisters—Fiction. 2. Geese—Fiction. 3. Behavior—Fiction.]
I. Greathouse, Justin, 1981- ill. II. Title.
PZ7.L8268Go 2008
[E]—dc22   2008006323

Gordon Grizwald's
Grumpy
Goose

by Nancy Loewen
illustrated by Justin Greathouse

Special thanks to our reading adviser:

Adria F. Klein, Ph.D.
Professor Emeritus, California State University
San Bernardino, California

PICTURE WINDOW BOOKS
Minneapolis, Minnesota

Gordon Grizwald's goose was a grump.

He never grinned a greeting. He never gabbed with the gang. He just glared and grunted. He grumbled and groaned.

5

"Give him some grain, Gordon," said Gordon's aunt Gladys.

So Gordon gathered some grain and gave it to the goose.

But the goose was still a grump. He never grinned a greeting. He never gabbed with the gang. He just glared and grunted. He grumbled and groaned.

"Would your goose like some grapes?" asked Granny Grizwald.

The grumpy goose glared.

"Grapefruit? Gravy? Gum?" Granny asked.

The grumpy goose glared and groaned.

"I give up," grumbled Granny. "Maybe your goose has gas."

"Maybe your grumpy goose is frightened,"
Gilbert Godfrey guessed.

"Golly, I don't think so," Gordon Grizwald said.

"Have any gorillas or ghosts gathered at your gate?" Gilbert asked.

"Good grief, no," Gordon Grizwald said.

Dr. Gomer Griffin gave Gordon Grizwald's
gloomy goose a check-up.

"Gosh," he said. "I don't know. The goose's guts are good. His glands are grand." The doctor grinned. "Get your goose to gargle with garlic. I'm guessing that your grump will get glad again."

13

So Gordon Grizwald's goose gargled garlic.

But it did no good. The goose was still a grump. He never grinned a greeting. He never gabbed with the gang. He just glared and grunted. He grumbled and groaned.

"I've got it!" said Gwen Glenn. "Your grumpy goose needs a gala!"

"A what?" asked Gordon Grizwald.

"A sparkly party," gushed Gwen Glenn. "I've got goose bumps just thinking about it!"

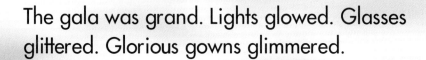

The gala was grand. Lights glowed. Glasses glittered. Glorious gowns glimmered.

"Well, grumpy goose?" asked Gwen Glenn. "Does my gala put a gleam in your eye?"

The grumpy goose growled.

Gwen Glenn's glow faded. "I give up," she said to her guests.

Then little Grace Grady stepped forward.

"Gordon Grizwald," the girl said, "your goose doesn't need grapes or gravy. He isn't scared of gorillas or ghosts. Gargling with garlic is nothing but gross! What your goose needs is some grass!"

21

The goose gave Grace Grady a grateful gaze.
The guests gasped. The girl guided the grumpy
goose into the grove.

"Go on," Grace Grady told the goose with a
grin. The goose giggled and began to graze.

From then on, Gordon Grizwald's goose always grinned a greeting. He often gabbed with the gang. He hardly ever glared or grunted, grumbled or groaned.

More *Read-it!* Readers

Bright pictures and fun stories help you practice your reading skills. Look for more books at your level.

Alex and the Team Jersey
Alex and Toolie
Another Pet
Betty and Baxter's Batter Battle
The Big Pig
Camden's Game
Cass the Monkey
Charlie's Tasks
Flora McQuack
Harold Hickok Had the Hiccups
Kyle's Recess

Marconi the Wizard
Peppy, Patch, and the Bath
Peter's Secret
Pets on Vacation
The Princess and the Tower
Sausages!
Theodore the Millipede
The Three Princesses
Tromso the Troll
Willie the Whale
The Zoo Band

On the Web

FactHound offers a safe, fun way to find Web sites related to topics in this book. All of the sites on FactHound have been researched by our staff.

1. Visit *www.facthound.com*

2. Type in this special code:
   1404848789

3. Click on the FETCH IT button.

Your trusty FactHound will fetch the best sites for you!
A complete list of *Read-it!* Readers is available on our Web site:
www.picturewindowbooks.com

24